The Cloud Story

A Bedtime Meditation for Children

Written by
Elliot A. Herland

Illustrated by
Kaitlyn J. Marquardt

Halo
PUBLISHING
INTERNATIONAL

Halo Publishing International
8000 W Interstate 10, #600
San Antonio, Texas 78230

First Edition, January 2023
Printed in the United States of America
ISBN: 978-1-63765-304-3
Library of Congress Control Number: 2022916410

Halo Publishing International is a self-publishing company that publishes adult fiction and non-fiction, children's literature, self-help, spiritual, and faith-based books. Do you have a book idea you would like us to consider publishing? Please visit www.halopublishing.com for more information.

To my children Evan, Lauren, Taylor, and Katy. You made me look forward to bedtime stories.

Remember.
Take a deep breath.

Hopping out on the gravel, we
run toward the brown-dirt path
lined with tall green grass.

Shallow puddles are here and there.

The air is filled with a sweet scent.

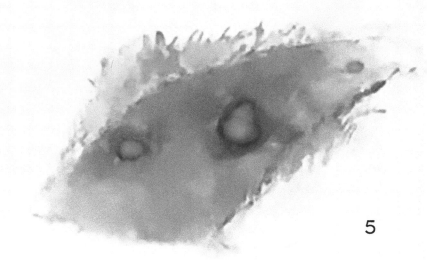

Dark-spotted leopard frogs peep and croak, then leap to hide in the grass.

The blue skies release a warm sunlight.

A single small, puffy cloud rests above as we reach the top of this special place and catch our breath.

Remember.
Take a deep breath.

A large tree grows there in the
middle of a clover-covered circle.

Its branches and twigs hold forests
of leaves. The sun shines through
them to touch the ground.

Let's sit in the shade
and sip in the cool air.

Cardinals and robins
are singing their songs.

They call to us, "Lie down, and
look up through the canopy!"

We breathe in through our noses
and then out of our mouths, slowly
stretching our bodies on top of the clover.

We look at each other's face and smile.

Remember.
Take a deep breath.

Soon, sleep slowly closes our eyes.

Gentle, cool breezes caress our faces
with a smooth, effortless touch.

They whisper, "Breathe deeply the fresh
air. Listen to the life all around us.
The stillness is yet to come."

The single small, puffy
cloud still rests above.

Opening our eyes wide, surrounded
by the blue sky, we're sitting on top
of the single small, puffy cloud!

The cloud takes us high
above the large tree!

Hold your breath!

Okay, now, you can let it out.

Slowly moving away from our tree, beneath us, there are turquoise ponds.

We see tall white birds fishing for their lunch under the dark-green lily pads.

Their beaks make the only splashes.

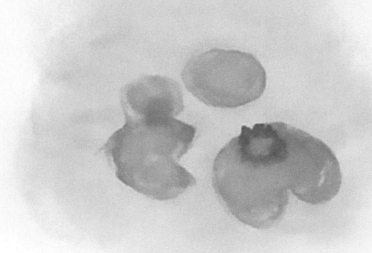

Remember.
Take a deep breath.

We move toward large, twisted oaks
and black-scarred white birch trees.

Squirrels chase each other across and
up the trunks, leaping from branches.

A woodpecker is busy pounding
for bugs with a *tap-tap, tap-tap*.

The sun warms our faces, but the air
cools as we deeply breathe it all in.

A mountain ahead, lined with bushes
and rocks, has a white cap glistening
of diamond-covered snow.

Crystal streams of water
flow from beneath it.

Up, up, up, we soar over the top,
holding in the cold air as we go
sliding down the other side.

Remember.
Take a deep breath.

We reach the lakeshore lined
with green and brown cattails.

Clear, clean water smooth as a glass
mirror reflects the blue sky that
stretches to the horizon ahead.

Ducks and geese glide on the water below
us, while fish and turtles swim deeper.

We sail as smoothly as the sand lying
deeper still at the bottom of the large lake.

On the opposite shore, a pine forest holds its secrets.

The deer are walking on golden tree-needle beds.

The blue jays are flying through brown branches.

The air is filled with the smell of sticky amber sap.

Remember.
Take a deep breath.

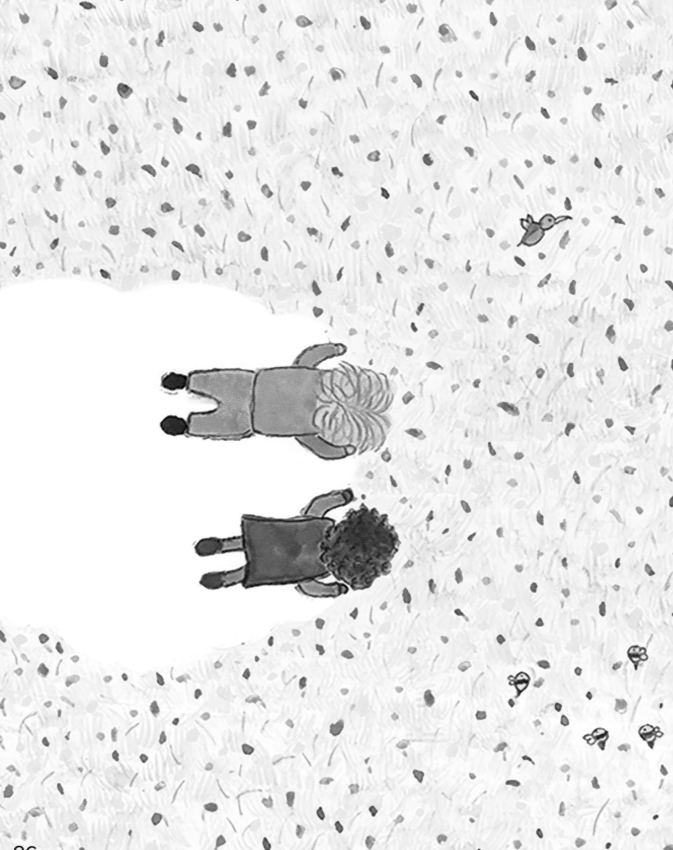

In the wildflower fields painted by
nature's own hand, we notice each
flower in the crowd of colors.

They softly say, "Breathe in our sweet
smell, and enjoy our many fragrances."

All around are honeybees and
hummingbirds kissing the petals
and savoring their life's work.

The single small, puffy cloud slows in the meadow and lays us down gently, tucking us into all of the colors, all of the sweet smells, all of the soft sounds, and under a blanket of blue sky still holding the sun's warmth.

Slowly, we let the air out of our chests.

Our eyes are closing now.

We begin to dream about all we remember.

We hopped out on the gravel.

We ran toward the brown-dirt path.

We reached the top of that special
place and caught our breath.

We saw the large tree in the middle
of a clover-covered circle.

We breathed in through our
noses and then out of our mouths.

We slowly stretched our
bodies on top of the clover.

We looked at each other's face.

We smiled.

The single small, puffy cloud rested above, waiting for us to fall asleep.

Take a deep breath, and remember.

CPSIA information can be obtained
at www.ICGtesting.com
Printed in the USA
LVHW070827250223
740155LV00034B/27